Take a Side

Written by Quinlan B. Lee

D1455462

LEGO, the LEGO logo, the Brick and Knob configurations and
© 2016 The LEGO Group. Produced by Scholastic

© & TM 2016 LUCASFILM LTD. Us

ISBN 978-0-545-91402-4

10 9 8 7 6 5 4 3 2 1   16 17 18 19 20

Printed in Malaysia   106

First printing 2016

Anakin **races** to tell **Mace** who the Sith Lord is.
"Is it too **late** to stop him?" he asks.
"We must **save** the day."

They **race** to find the Sith Lord.
"**Take** it easy, **Mace**,"
says Anakin.
"I am not in good **shape**
like you."

"Nice **cape**," **Mace** says.
"You are too **late**!" the
Sith Lord says.
"The **fate** of the Jedi
is bad.
You can not **save** them."

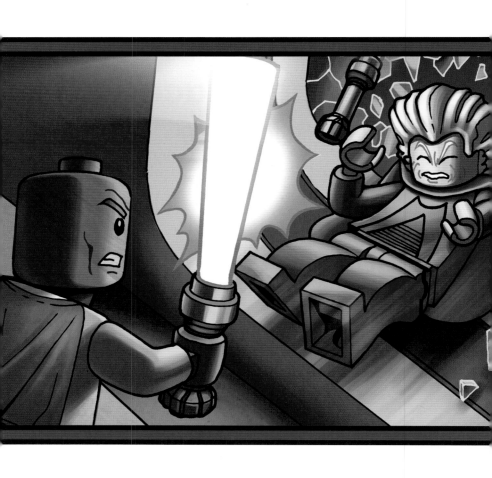

"Why would you **change** sides?" says **Mace**.
"The dark side is **lame**."
He swings his **saber**.
"**Take** that, you **snake**!"

"**Wait**!" yells Anakin.
"He is not that bad.
And I kind of like
his **cape**."
"It is too **late**," says
Mace.
"I am going to **take**
him out!"

"No, YOU are too **late**," says the Sith Lord. He blasts **Mace**. "I cannot **shake** it," **Mace** says. "The dark side is more than I can **take**."

"Whose side should I **take**?" asks Anakin. "*Hmmm* . . . the Jedi **make** me **race** all over the **place**. And the Sith Lord has that cool **cape** . . . I think I'll **take** the dark side."

Anakin **makes** his choice
He **changes** sides. He
gets a **cape**, too.